This Library Card Belongs To:

Insert
Picture
Here

_____

I promise to return these books

DEDICATION

To my wonderful mother—thank you for every dollar given to my hopeful eyes at the Scholastic Book Fair, and countless hours at the public library

To my wife—for always being a pair of fresh eyes and a beacon when doubt creeps in

To Andi—for being the sounding board and mentor every creative deserves

To Mrs. McMahon—whose English class unlocked the writer within me

And to the lovely librarians at the Monroe Library—who issued my first library card that allowed me to take adventures within their walls every day after school

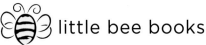 little bee books

New York, NY
Copyright © 2022 by Tiffany Rose
All rights reserved, including the right of reproduction in whole or in part in any form.
Manufactured in China RRD 0921
First Edition
10 9 8 7 6 5 4 3 2 1
Library of Congress Cataloging-in-Publication Data is available upon request.
ISBN 978-1-4998-1225-1
littlebeebooks.com
For information about special discounts on bulk purchases,
please contact Little Bee Books at sales@littlebeebooks.com.

Tiffany Rose

Dear Reader

A Love Letter to Libraries

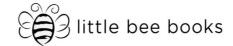
little bee books

Dear Reader, do you see that little girl down there? That's me with the big hair, the one surrounded by all the books. Look!

I devour so many books, I prefer them to meals.
Books for breakfast, lunch, and dinner—with a side of adventure,
and heavy on the feels, please!

Big books,
small books,
thin books,
and tall books.

Books about fish, alligators,
science, and shells.
Books full of thrones, quests,
friendship, and dreams.

Books with brave heroines and heroes saving the day,
overcoming every obstacle set in their way.

I think of myself as a heroine, too.

In my cat ears, knee socks, and my favorite green shorts, I'm ready to take on the world!

From page to page, characters can become
my best friends and make my heart soar,
or they can become worthy adversaries
to defeat with a clever plan.

Even after spending all day
in the library with them,
I always want more . . .
and more . . . and more.

There was just this one thing, this nagging suspicion,
that I didn't meet the criteria for a heroine's condition.

In the books that I read, an absence of melanin was a clear omission.

I looked at all the books that I loved, but could not remember a single, solitary character that looked like myself in any of these different stories and fantastical worlds.

This must be a mistake, an oversight, a snafu, a misprint.

So back to the library I went,
searching for characters of the same hue.
And all I found were books of
struggle, hardship, and pain.

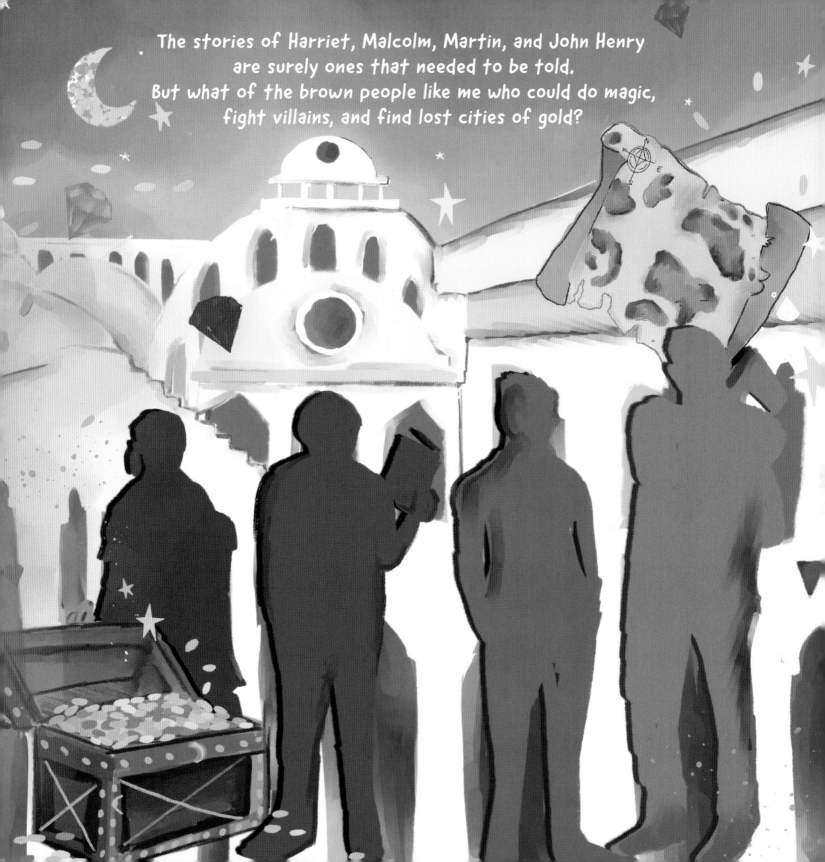

The stories of Harriet, Malcolm, Martin, and John Henry
are surely ones that needed to be told.
But what of the brown people like me who could do magic,
fight villains, and find lost cities of gold?

What did that mean for a girl like me,
who felt the call of destiny
that all great stories provide,

to never see a face like mine,
inked on the pages inside?

It didn't make me love the stories I'd read any less.
But now, I want more, *need* more.

Cocoa-colored mer-people,
honey-hued dragon slayers,

and superheroes with locs.
Afro puffs on other planets,

and a heroine who thinks
outside of the box.

I once read that if the path you want doesn't exist, create it.

So that's just what I'll do.

And then Taneisha tamed the lion with her magical scarf. A rainbow of colors bursting into a spectrum of threads, each one Float... the air. ...Taneisha her ...less scarf

I'll put pen to paper. Make my melanated words come to life.
I'll tell stories of imagination, magic, and adventure,
then set them on the shelf next to our ones of pain and strife.

It'll say my name right there on the spine.
Populating every shelf, letting kids who look like me shine.

With one turn of the page,
you'll be whisked away to far-off lands.

I can tumble down rabbit holes,
set sail upon ruby-colored seas,
and take twilight tea with a djinni.

Tangled in long seaweed locs and an abundance of words,
I imagine worlds beyond the one we live in. And you can, too.

Scribbling away, stories pour out of me all day and night.

Stories so that children who look like me can see themselves exploring and saving and discovering and creating.

Daring to do the impossible
as their imagination takes flight.

Our stories are as diverse as our skin and deserve to be told.

So pick up a book or a pen—

and let the magic unfold!